A Finger had a hand in it, too.

Bill

THE BOY WONDER

THE SECRET CO-CREATOR OF BATMAN

Marc Tyler Nobleman
Illustrated by **Ty Templeton**

Charlesbridge

To Charles, Lyn, and Athena, who respectively revealed the soul, heart, and hope of Bill Finger—M. T. N.

To my father, Charles, who started *his* life as a cartoonist; Bill Finger, who started *my* life as a cartoonist; and my wife, Keiren, who sustains my life, whether I'm cartooning or not—T. T.

This book is about getting deserved credit. Another round of thanks goes to the following: Lyn Simmons; Charles Sinclair and Gayle Sanders; Jerry Robinson; Athena Finger; Judy Flam; Eric Flam; Gerard Pelisson; Darren Turco; Deana Fagan; Burton J. Finger; Beverly Manasch; Bonnie Burrell; Nancy H. Cole; Alvin Schwartz; Tom Andrae; Jerry Bails; Tom Fagan; Joe Latino; Eve Simmons; Steven J. Simmons; Jim Amash; Arnold Drake; Roy Thomas; Sean Stevenson; Bob Hughes; John Wells; Kevin Miller; Marc Svensson; Anthony Tollin; Bob Brodsky; Florence Liberman; Irwin Hasen; Carmine Infantino; Mike W. Barr; Teriananda; Josh Peterson; Philomena Ivezic; Lou Mougin; Bill Wormstedt; Will Murray; Mai Qaraman; Sheila Kieval; Jordan Auslander; Eileen Polakoff; Vanessa Foreman; Lancelot McGough; Jean Bails; Bill Schelly; Aaron Caplan; Bill Schelly; Ray Feighery; Gerard Jones; Larry Goldman; Herb Goldman; Paul A. and Harriet Finger; Lorna Sinclair-Wood; Cory Sinclair; Kimberly Sinclair; Dolly Alevizatos; Jon Gelchinsky; Leonard Grossman; Colleen Kurka; Aggie Moskowitz; Dave Weiss; Bob Perkins; Shelly Moldoff; Lew Sayre Schwartz; Joe Kubert; Jerry Stephan; David Tosh; Marybelle Vals; Linda Wood; Joe Desris; Art Shenkin; Bud Shenkin; Mark Waid; Mariano Bayona Estradera; Paul Kupperberg; David Siegel; Bitsy Proler; Julien Rosenthal; Edward Greene; Dwight Jon Zimmerman; Mark Evanier; Michael Uslan; Jim Ashcraft; Ines Ferdenzi; Dennis O'Neil; Dwight Finger; Paul T. Finger; Nan Kaplan; Liz Wissner-Gross; Dave Kraft; Mark S. Zaid; Sean Walsh; Alan J. Porter; Joe Azzato; Lila Baltman; Charlie Roberts; Jackie Estrada; Bruce Mason; Scott Tipton; Mike Scott; Jacqueline Richardson; Will Brooker; Mike Catron; Maggie Thompson; Paula Simon; Gale Grant; Lloyd Ultan; Chris Marshall; Gary Colabuono; Jason Claud; Craig Delich; Craig Byrne; Alan Gammill; Neil Polowin; Thomas Ganes; Irina Zaionts; Patricia O'Byrne; Bill Jourdain; A. David Lewis; Susan Holtzman; Anne Diamond; Judith McQuown; Tracy Manasch Williams; Bill's sister, Emily; Christian Campagnuolo; Seth Kessler; Andrew Douglas; Caryn Wiseman; Alyssa Mito Pusey (her championing this book made her my champion) and the team at Charlesbridge (brave and bold all); Mom, Dad, and Darby; my dynamic duo, Lara and Rafael; and Daniela, who, like Bill Finger, has been a savvy and selfless behind-the-scenes creative partner of incalculable value.—M. T. N.

Published by Charlesbridge
85 Main Street
Watertown, MA 02472
(617) 926-0329
www.charlesbridge.com

Library of Congress Cataloging-in-Publication Data
Nobleman, Marc Tyler.
    Bill the boy wonder : the secret co-creator of Batman / Marc Tyler Nobleman ; illustrated by Ty Templeton.
        p. cm.
    ISBN 978-1-58089-289-6 (reinforced for library use)
1. Finger, Bill, 1914–1974—Juvenile literature. 2. Cartoonists—United States—Biography—Juvenile literature.
3. Batman (Comic strip)—Juvenile literature. I. Templeton, Ty. II. Title.
PN6727.F495Z75 2012
741.5'973—dc23 [B]   2011025695

Printed in China
(hc) 10 9 8 7 6 5 4 3 2 1

Illustrations created on 30-lb. bond paper, inked with Faber-Castell artist pens, and colored in Photoshop
Display type and text type set in Atomic Wedgie, Block Berthold, and Aldine 401 BT
Color separations by KHL Chroma Graphics, Singapore
Printed and bound February 2012 by Jade Productions in Heyuan, Guangdong, China
Production supervision by Brian G. Walker
Designed by Martha MacLeod Sikkema

After Milton Finger graduated from high school, he invented his first secret identity.

In 1933 Jews were sometimes not hired just because they were Jews. *Milton* was commonly a Jewish name, so Milton chose a new one: *Bill*.

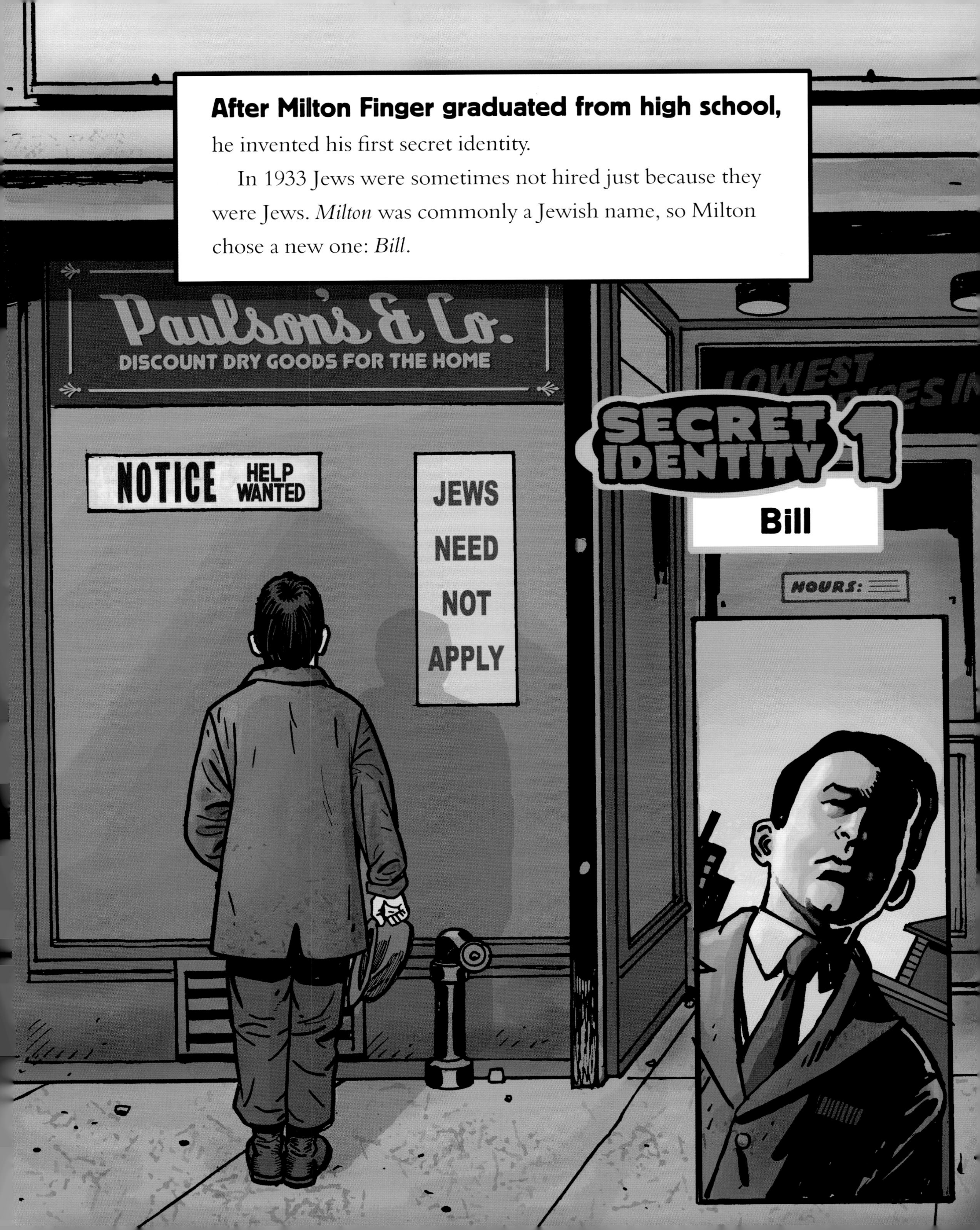

Paulson's & Co.
DISCOUNT DRY GOODS FOR THE HOME
NOTICE HELP WANTED
JEWS NEED NOT APPLY
LOWEST
SECRET IDENTITY 1
Bill
HOURS:

During the Great Depression Bill's father was forced to close his Bronx tailor shop. The family was struggling, so Bill took any job he could get, one after the other—and disliked them all.

Bill's parents had pressured him to become a doctor.

Bill wanted to be an artist and a writer.

In early 1939 he was a shoe salesman.

Bill loved literature—and he had ideas. He'd shared some of them with Bob Kane, a cartoonist he'd met at a party. Bob was so wowed that he asked Bill to write adventure stories for him to illustrate. They collaborated on a couple of comic-book features that did get published but didn't get much attention.

Superman had debuted the year before and was a smash from the start. One Friday Vin Sullivan, an editor at the company that would become DC Comics, told Bob that he wanted another superhero sensation.

Bob said he'd have one by Monday.

That weekend he sketched but felt that the character wasn't coming together. He needed help. As for who was the man for the job, he put his Finger on it right away.

Bob hightailed it to Bill's Bronx apartment.

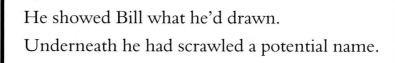

He showed Bill what he'd drawn.
Underneath he had scrawled a potential name.

The BAT-MAN

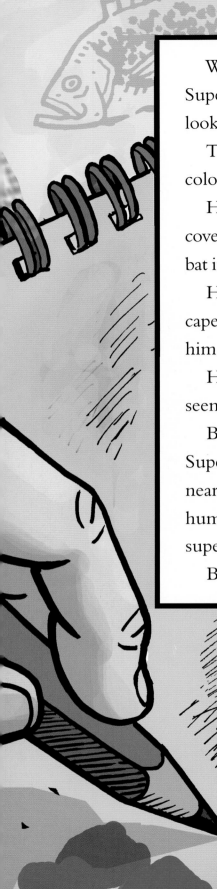

Wings aside, Bob's design reminded Bill too much of Superman. Bill figured a character named after a bat should look menacing—even though he would be a good guy.

The red union suit struck Bill as too cheery. He proposed colors that could better fade into the shadows.

He recommended replacing the wisp of a mask with a cowl that covered all but Bat-Man's chin. Pointing out an illustration of a bat in a dictionary, he said, "Why don't we duplicate the ears?"

He felt that the wings were awkward. "I suggest you make a cape and scallop the edges," Bill said. "It would flow out behind him when he runs and *look* like bat wings."

He thought Bat-Man would be more intimidating if it seemed that he had no pupils—just white slits for eyes.

Bill knew that Bat-Man should not only look different from Superman but also *be* different. Superman was alien-born and near-invulnerable. Bill thought that Bat-Man should be a human being who could be hurt. A superhero without superpowers. Someone anyone could be.

Bob liked Bill's changes.

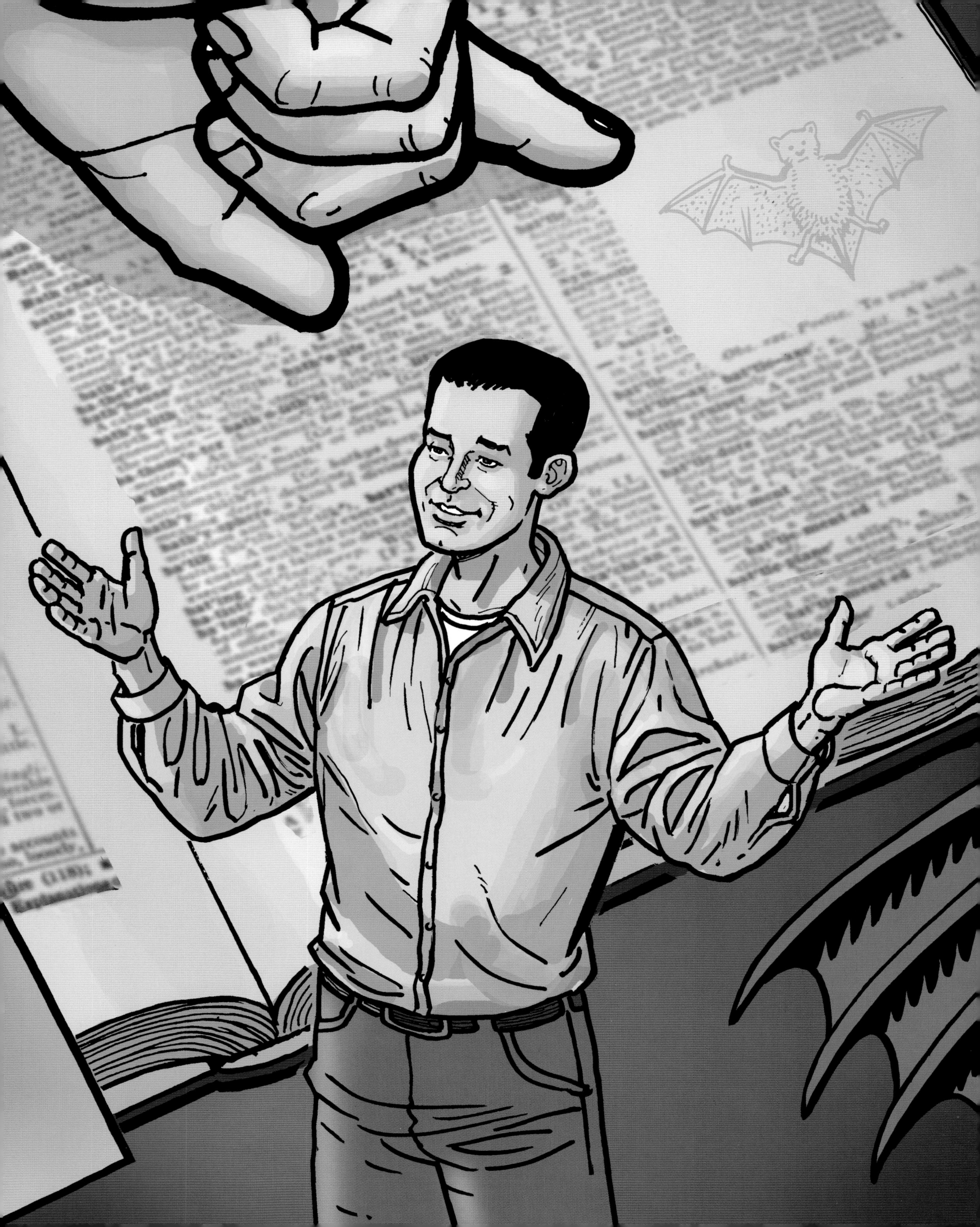

Come Monday, Bob indeed had a superhero for Vin—
though the superhero's name was about all that remained
of Bob's concept. Bob showed Bat-Man to Vin—without Bill.
Vin promptly wanted to run Bat-Man, and Bob negotiated
a deal—without including Bill. Bat-Man had Bill's Fingerprints
all over him, yet Vin did not know there *was* a Bill.

Bob told Bill that Bat-Man would be published and asked Bill to write it—without credit. Because such an arrangement was fairly typical, and because writing gigs were tough to get, but mainly because Bill was an agreeable sort, he said yes.

With that, Bill took on his second secret identity.

However, he would soon realize that he had been blind about this Bat.

SECRET IDENTITY 2

Writer of Batman

In April 1939 Bat-Man flitted onto newsstands as the lead feature in *Detective Comics #27*. Bill's writing style was influenced by trashy pulp magazines and classy novels, comic strips and cinema. He fused it all into a type of character that readers had not seen before—a hero who looked like a villain, a vigilante who was also a detective.

Bill and Bob would sit in Poe Park, named for Edgar Allan Poe, father of the modern detective story. Close to the cottage where Poe had lived nearly a century before, the duo would brainstorm detective stories of their own.

Though Bill had wanted Bat-Man to differ from Superman, Bat-Man instantly copied Superman in a most welcome way: the dark knight was a white-hot hit.

At age twenty-five Bill no longer had to be a shoe salesman or anything anyone else wanted him to be. *Bat-Man* became *Batman*, and Bill became a full-time—if modestly paid and anonymous—writer.

No. 34   THE BATMAN   DECEMBER

Detecti

COMI

Almost immediately Bob hired other artists to do the drawing—and insisted that they, too, work anonymously. Among the first was a gifted seventeen-year-old named Jerry Robinson. Between deadlines Bill and Jerry saw foreign films and played darts. Jerry knew Bill was increasingly troubled that Bob claimed all the credit for Batman.

But Bill stuck with it. Now that Batman had caught on, he needed to come up with an origin for him. He asked himself what could drive a man to dress as a giant winged mammal and protect strangers from evil every night. He arrived at a horrific answer.

A young boy stands by helplessly as a mugger shoots his parents to death and gets away. The boy vows to prevent other people from suffering as he has. For years he trains his mind and body until both are in peak condition. As an adult he dons a grim costume and patrols the streets to strike terror into the superstitious, cowardly hearts of criminals.

Before Bill, comic-book characters saved lives simply because they were born heroes. Bill was the first writer to saddle a superhero with an emotional reason to wage war on crime.

Through grief and rage, Batman was *made* a hero.

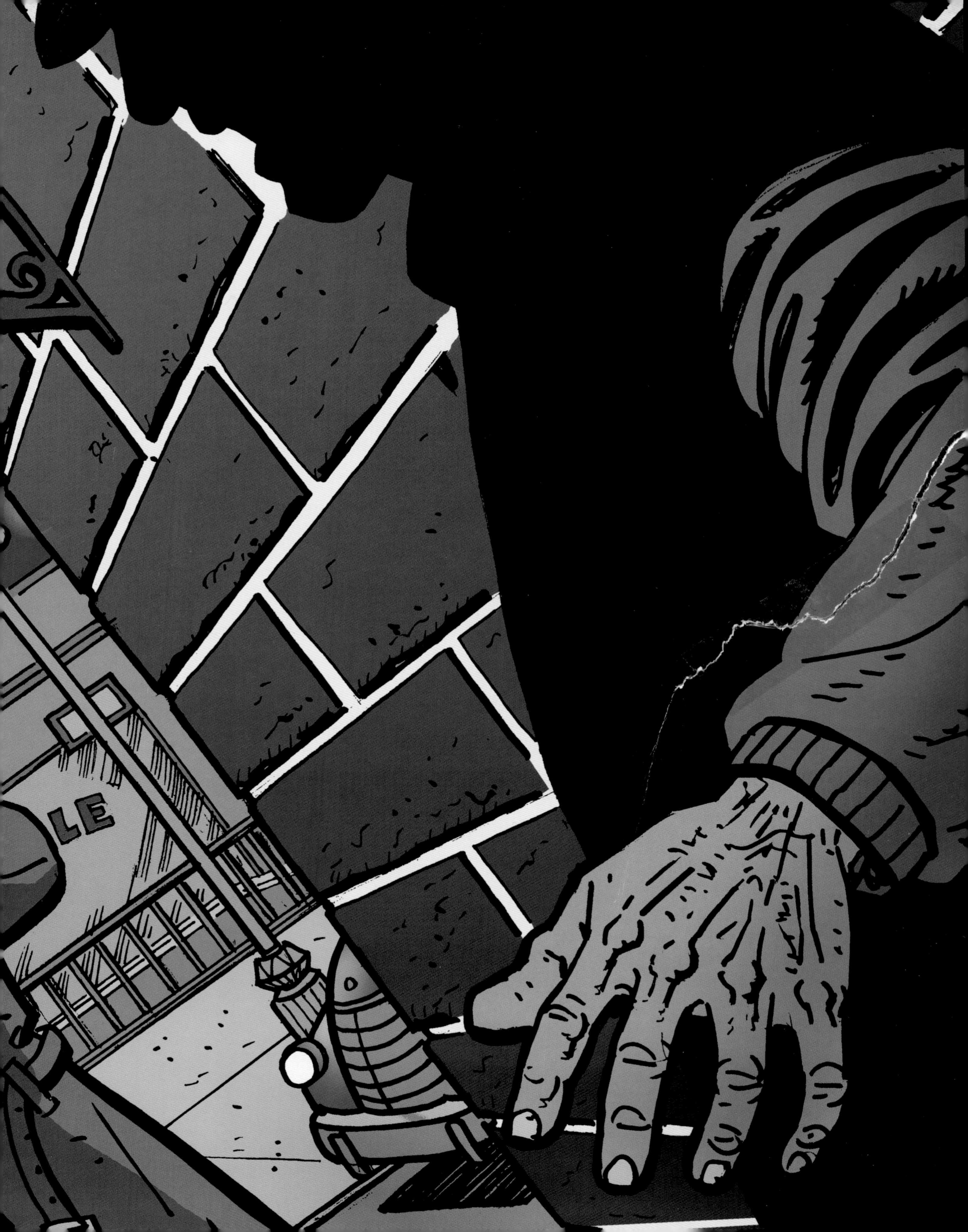
LE

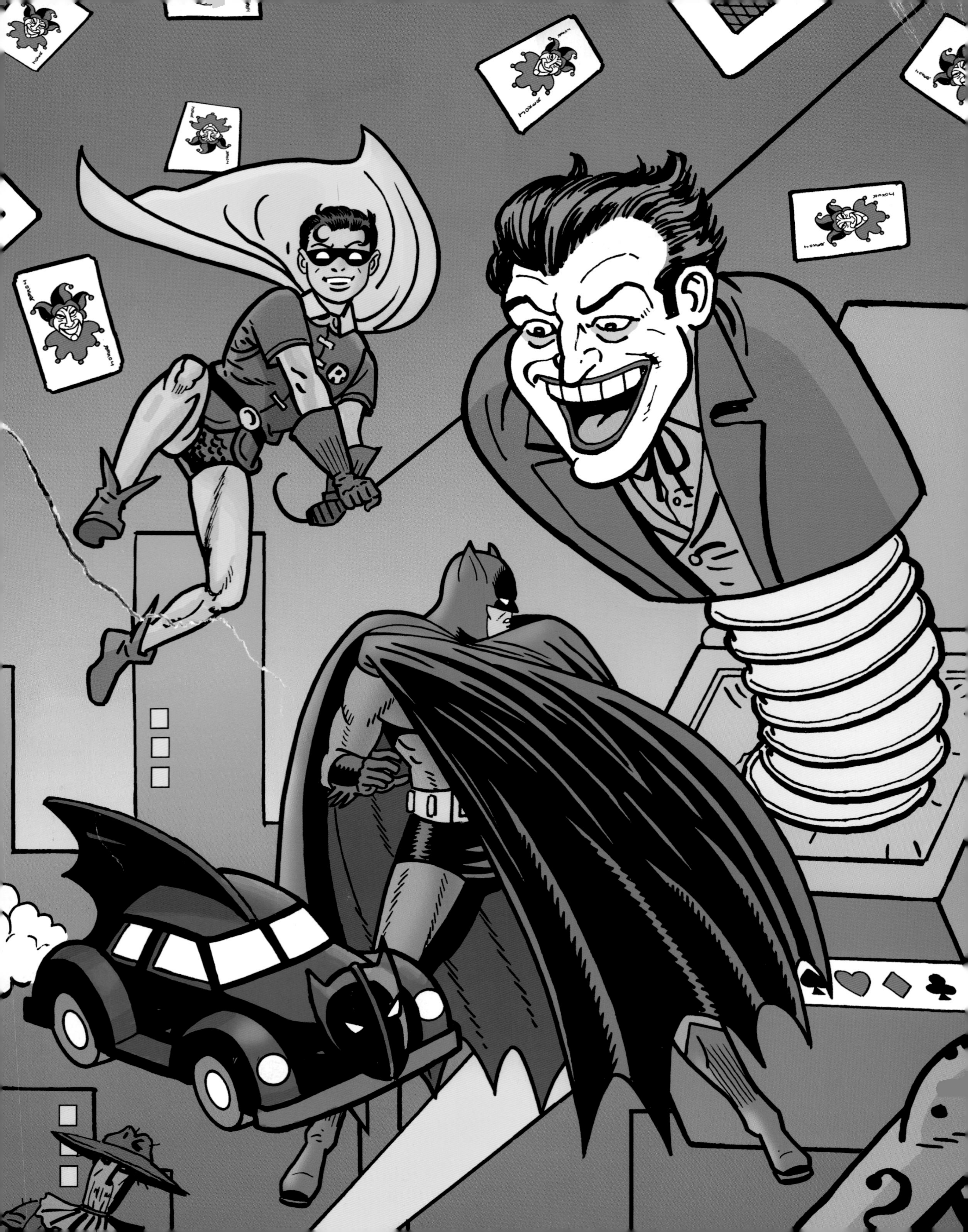

Steadily, silently, Bill built a vivid world around Batman. Knowing from secret identities, he'd given Batman one: wealthy heir Bruce Wayne. Bill dubbed Batman's city Gotham after seeing the word in the phone book. He called Batman's car the Batmobile and his underground base the Batcave. Bill was an idea factory. Bob called him a "boy wonder."

"Batman doesn't have anyone to talk to," Bill said. So another boy wonder was born—a partner in crime busting (and fellow orphan) named Robin. Young readers who had imagined they could be Batman when they grew up now imagined they could be Robin *tomorrow*. Sales doubled. Heroes in other comics recruited their own kid sidekicks.

In 1940 Batman got his own comic. In the first issue he confronted a killer clown named the Joker and a beguiling burglar who became known as Catwoman. Bill concocted memorable rogues almost as regularly as some people compiled grocery lists.

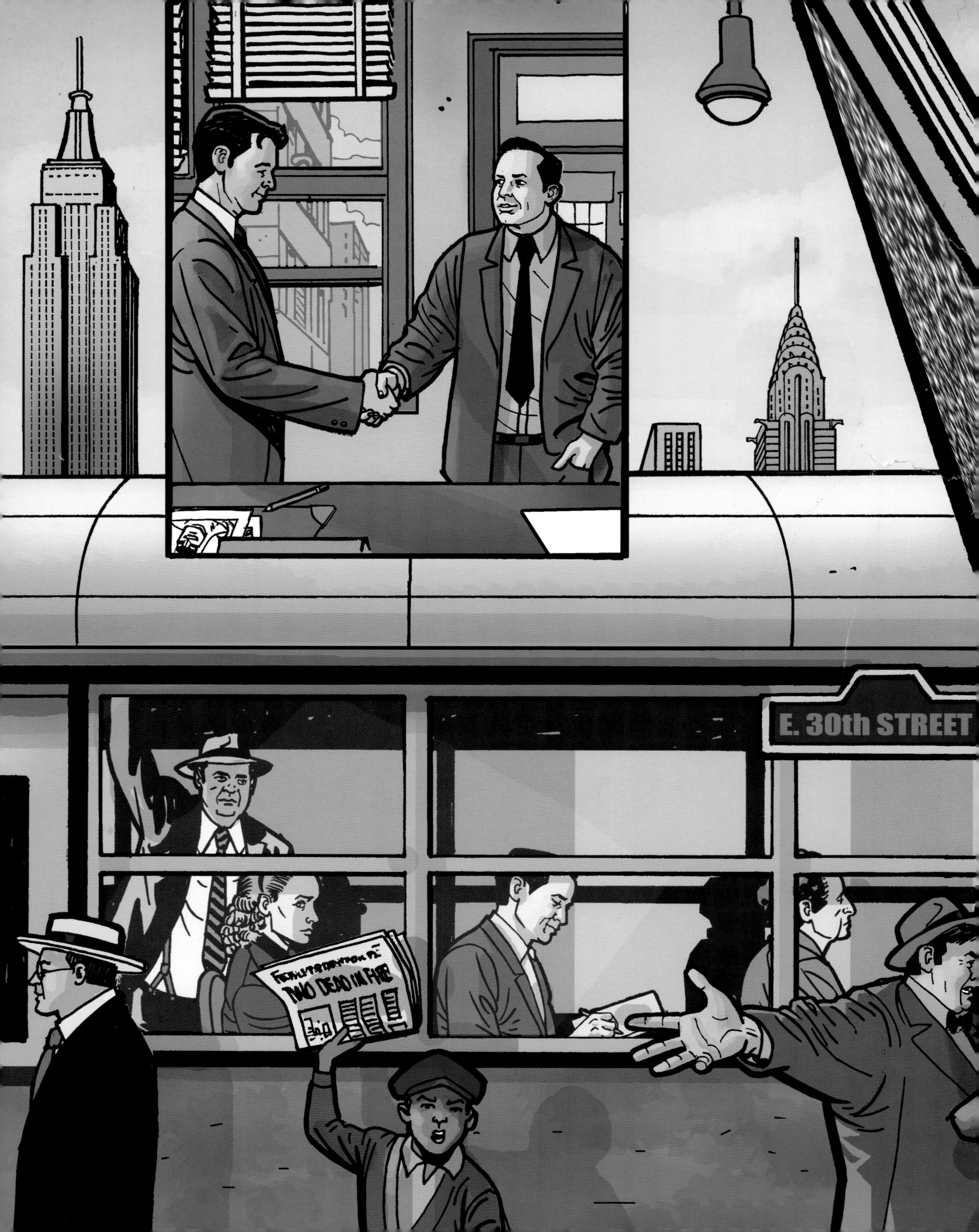
E. 30th STREET
TWO DEAD IN FIRE

Other comics creators were so impressed with Bill's talent that they couldn't keep his secret. They told editors that he, not Bob, was writing Batman. Thrilled, editors began giving Bill assignments directly. Both Bill and Bob kept working on Batman. The difference was that Bill no longer worked *for* Bob.

Bill liked to ride through the city to think. As the bus picked up passengers, Bill picked up plots from street scenes and daydreams.

He recorded stray facts—the boiling point of mercury, the Chinese character for *virtue*, what happens when a dog's nose gets cold—in what he called his "gimmick book." He routinely skimmed it for a spark that might ignite a story. In time he had a library of gimmick books at his Fingertips. He even let other writers—his competitors—hunt for story ideas in them.

"achluophobia"
a fear of
the dark

Virtue

德

time zones
established
by railroads
1883

In 1948 Bill and his wife, Portia, had their only child. They named him Fred. Bill called him "Little Finger." Bill took Fred on weekend expeditions to the zoo or the planetarium. When Fred was still below the minimum age allowed to enter the American Museum of Natural History, Bill snuck him in.

While his son was getting an education around town, Bill was collecting more gems for the gimmick book. "In every person there is something that says, 'I'd like to return to the innocence of my childhood,'" Bill said. To capture that, he sometimes asked Fred for his opinion on scripts.

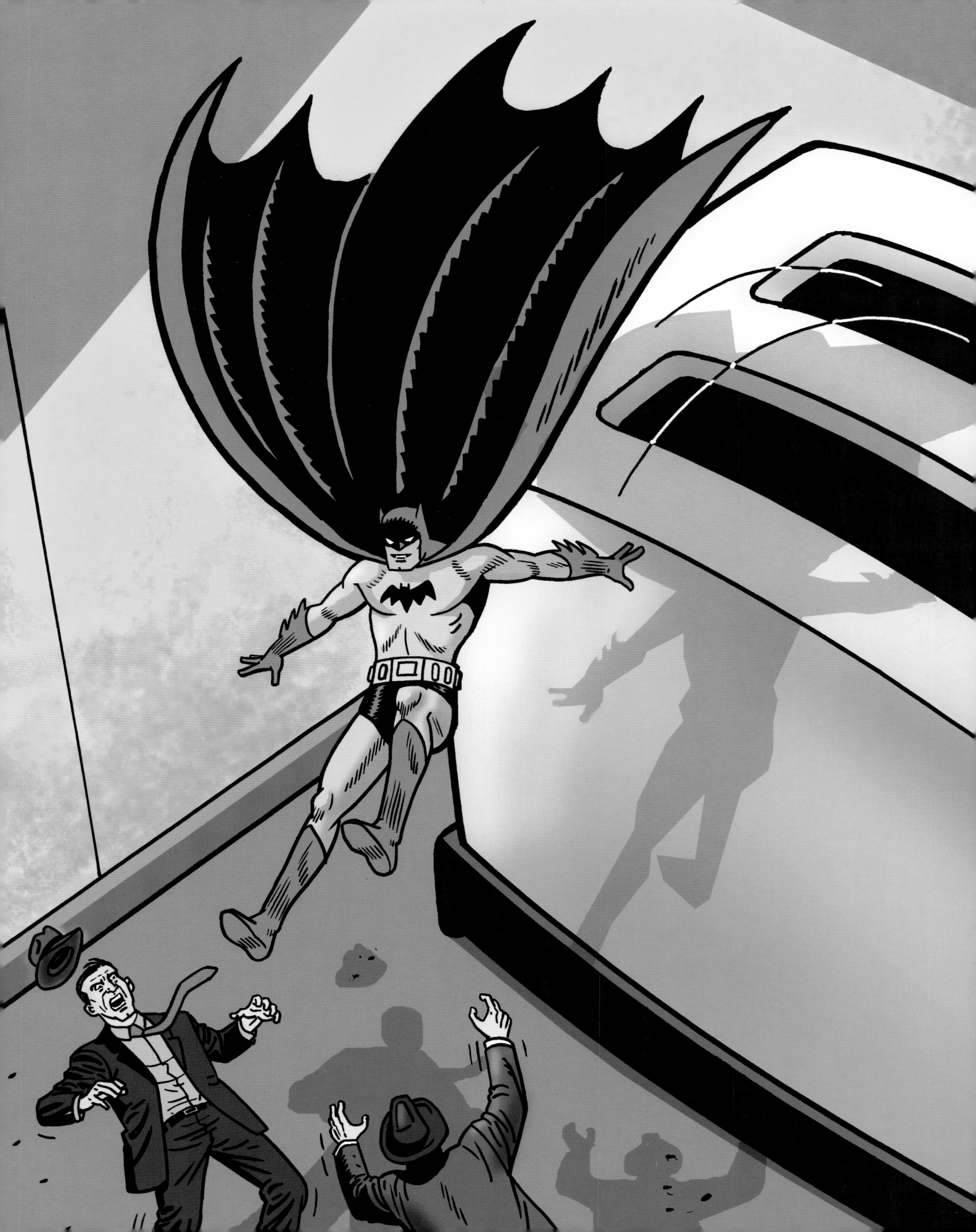

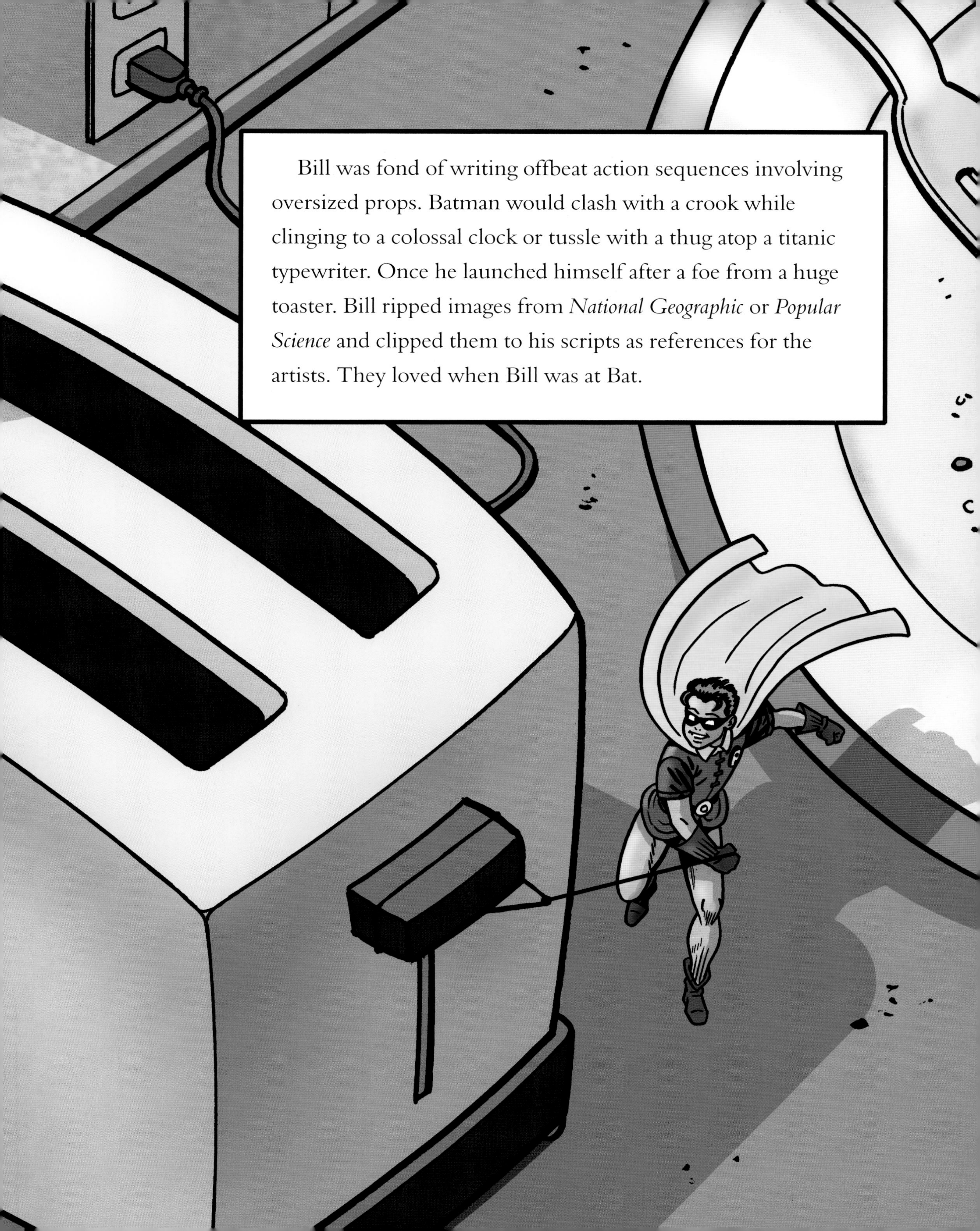

Bill was fond of writing offbeat action sequences involving oversized props. Batman would clash with a crook while clinging to a colossal clock or tussle with a thug atop a titanic typewriter. Once he launched himself after a foe from a huge toaster. Bill ripped images from *National Geographic* or *Popular Science* and clipped them to his scripts as references for the artists. They loved when Bill was at Bat.

To get his stories just right, Bill worked long days and sometimes, like Batman, all night. (*Not* like Batman, he fueled up on chicken soup to get through the wee hours.)

But Bill's gimmick-gathering and art-accumulating research methods often took more time than he was supposed to use. If Bill told someone he had a script due on Monday, it probably meant *last* Monday. Some editors put up with Bill's lateness because his stories turned out so crackerjack. Others could be cruel, yelling at Bill in front of his peers.

DUE:
SEPT 20TH

During the first twenty-five years of Batman comics, Bill's name appeared in one only once—sort of. A 1943 story depicted a poster for a concert by musicians Regnif and Enak—*Finger* and *Kane* backward. Bob never offered Bill a byline. Bill may have asked for one at some point, but he had not pushed. Though Bill's colleagues considered him the best comic-book writer of his generation, his identity was still a secret to Batmanians (as fans were called).

In 1964 that changed. Comics editor Julius Schwartz started to spill about Bill. He announced that a fellow named Finger had written "most of the classic Batman adventures of the past two decades."

The next summer New York City hosted the first large-scale comic convention. Bill and three others spoke on the first-ever panel of comics creators. The panel moderator was a longtime Batman fan named Jerry Bails. He introduced Bill as the creator of many characters and as "a Batman writer from the very first."

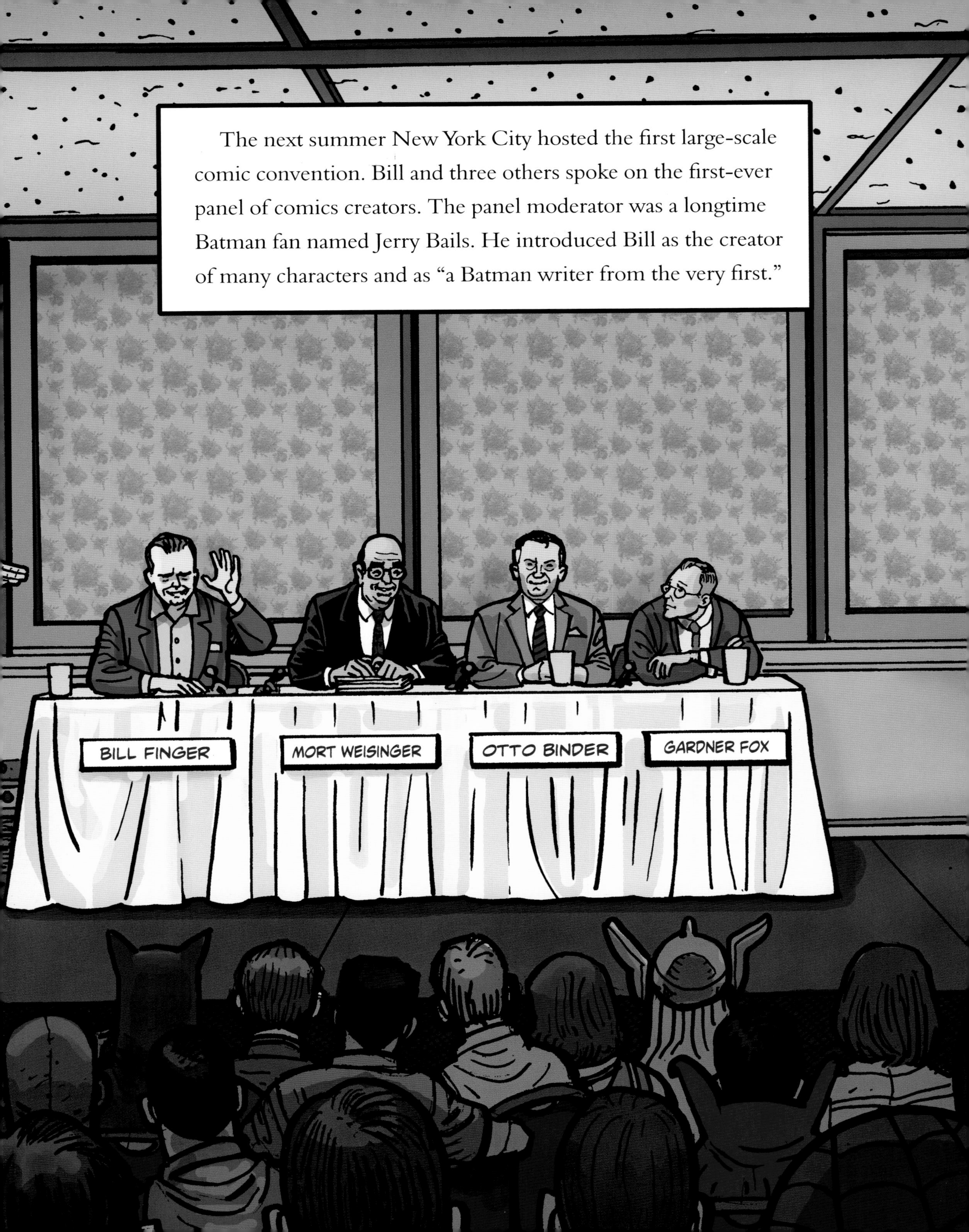
BILL FINGER
MORT WEISINGER
OTTO BINDER
GARDNER FOX

Jerry also did his own detective work about his detective hero. The same summer as the convention, he interviewed Bill about the beginning of Batman. And for the first time on record, Bill revealed that he had done more on Batman than write stories.

Later that year Jerry put out an article based on the interview. And so fans learned Bill's *third* secret identity—his role in *creating* Batman.

SECRET IDENTITY 3

Co-creator of Batman

IF THE TRUTH BE K

OR

"A Finger in Every

Somewhere today in Greenwich Village the
of notepaper; tucked away in a desk draw
mentos, it is mute testimony of a famous epis
of the man who gave life to Comic
The episode? The birth o
given to the Cowl
both sides
snapp
g as
trade
sn't
cters
he h
Beh

Bob publicly accused Bill of exaggerating. Despite that,
Batmanians believed Bill. They began to murmur that he
should be credited as the co-creator of Batman—that this Bill
was long past due. But Bill *still* didn't push. He could write great
fights but could not seem to fight for himself.

in the
typer of Bill Fing

Bill is an unassuming man, who was, his
to recognize his talent for writing for th
conist Bob Kane was the first to
Bill to write "Rusty an
uccess, Bill be

Bill's final Batman comic-book story went on sale in late 1965. In the early 1970s he began writing stories for mystery comics.

On the morning of Friday, January 18, 1974, Bill owed DC Comics two scripts, but turned in only one. He assured the editor he'd have the other story on Monday.

Come Monday, there *was* a Bill Finger story, but not the one the editor—or anyone else—wanted.

That Friday afternoon, a month shy of his sixtieth birthday, Bill had passed away in his sleep.

Now grown, Fred brought his father's ashes to a beach.
He arranged them on the sand in a fitting shape.

The tide crept in and swept them out to sea.

Bill died knowing Batman was one of only two superheroes to be published monthly without interruption since the 1930s (Superman being the other). He died having seen "Story by Bill Finger" begin to run on reprints of his early Batman work. But it was mostly after he was gone that fans went to bat for Bill, urging DC to acknowledge him as co-creator.

In a publication that came out shortly after Bill's death, the publisher of DC stated that Batman had lost "one of his two real fathers." In another, DC ran a full-page drawing of Batman bowing his head at a gravestone for Bill and a summary of his career that ended, "Few men have contributed as much to comics as Bill Finger."

In Bob's later years he showed a side few if any had seen before. "Bill never received the fame and recognition he deserved," he said in 1989. "If I could go back . . . before he died, I would like to say, 'I'll put your name on it now. You deserve it.'"

But Bob didn't amend the part of his contract requiring that he always be listed as the sole creator of Batman.

Jerry Robinson had long wanted a high-profile way to pay tribute to his old friend. He led the establishment of an award to honor past and present writers who greatly enriched the art of comic-book storytelling. The award did not go to Bill.

CREATED BY

BOB KANE

It was named after him.

In 2005 the first annual Bill Finger Awards for Excellence in Comic Book Writing were given out.

Today Bill Finger continues to inspire comics creators. Like Bruce Wayne, they vow to fight for justice—their own. They refuse to let what happened to Bill happen to them.

From Milton to Bill, from salesman to Batman, from secret co-creator to unsung legend, Bill's most important story was not one he wrote but the one he lived. Will his name ever be added to every Batman story?

Batmanians are keeping their Fingers crossed.

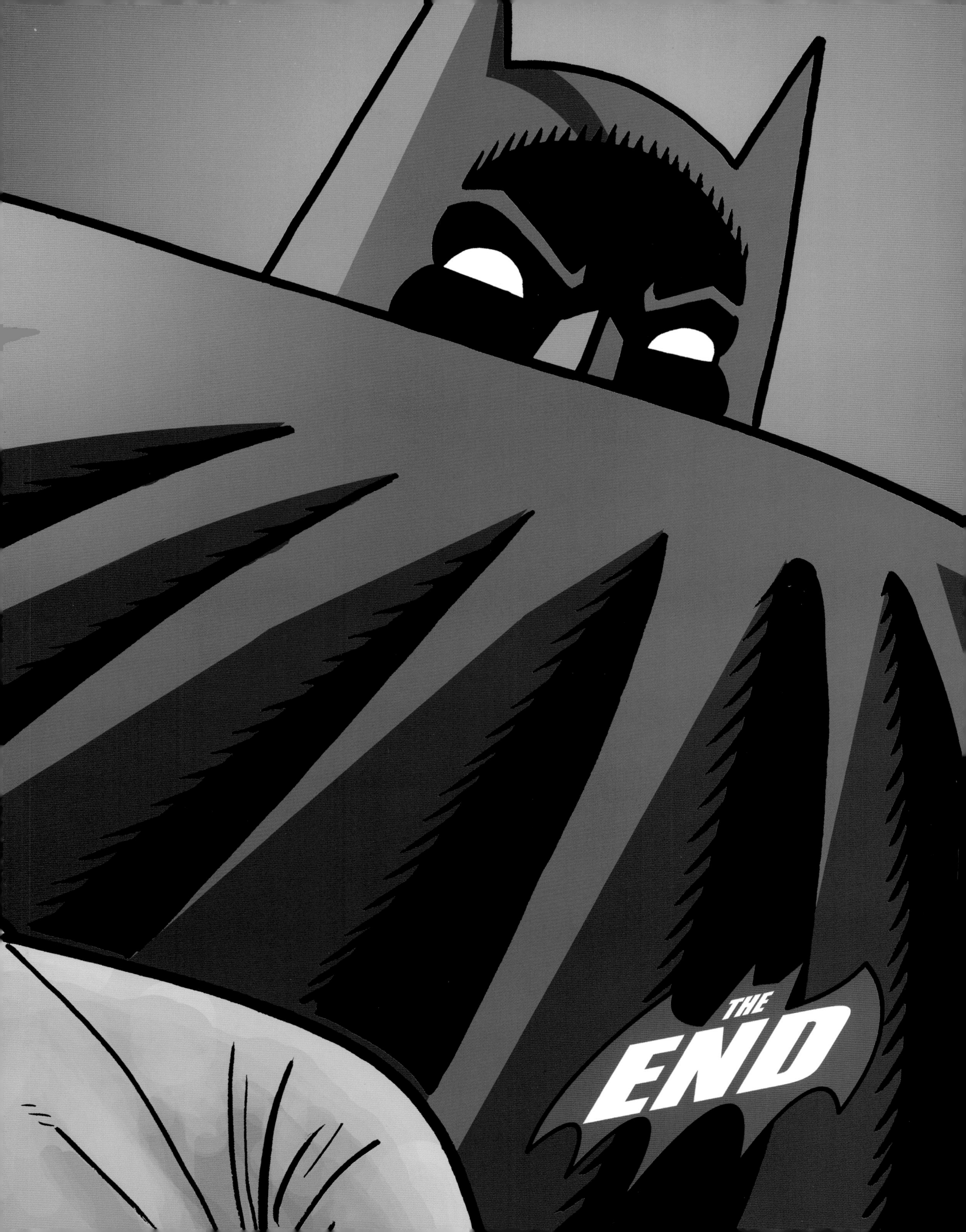
THE
END

Author's Note

The Father of Batman

The last line in the first panel of the first Batman story refers to Batman, but for at least a quarter century, it also applied to the man who wrote it: "His identity remains unknown."

Considering Bill Finger was the prime mind behind Batman—one of the most iconic characters in pop-culture history—it's startling how little has been written about him. No obituary for Bill ran in the mainstream media. He has not been the focus of a book before.

Until I began to dig, a lot of the little we knew about Bill was thanks to Jerry Bails, the enterprising comics fan and independent publisher who died in 2006. His pivotal 1965 interview, in which Bill explained just how much he'd done at the dawn of Batman, resulted in a fanzine article called "If the Truth Be Known or 'A Finger in Every Plot!'"

In response Bob Kane pointed the Finger at Bill in a letter published in another fanzine, *Batmania*. Bob challenged Bill to repeat the claims to his face. He proclaimed, "I, Bob Kane, am the sole creator of 'Batman.'"

After reading Bob's *Batmania* letter, Bill promptly called Bob. "I quite angrily spoke my mind and jogged Bob's fading memory," Bill wrote in a personal letter. It may be the only indication in print that Bill—at least once—did stand up to Bob.

Though Bill apparently didn't lobby for official credit or more money, he did continue to correct the record. In 1970 Bill stated that it was he who named Bruce Wayne and Gotham City. (The origin of the Joker is a subject of ongoing debate. Bob said that he and Bill created him. Jerry Robinson said that *he* and Bill created him. The constant was Bill—no one disputes that he wrote the first Joker story.)

In an interview conducted in 1972, Bill was perhaps more incriminating than in any other known documented instance. Reflecting on his quarter-century of work on Batman, he said, "Bob Kane was using me as a kind of tool all this time, to bolster his own paycheck."

In his 1989 autobiography, *Batman & Me*, Bob included a sketch of a Batman-like figure conspicuously dated 1934—five years before Bob went to Bill for brainstorming. Bob said that, in 1939, he'd "remembered" the sketch. He seemed to want to prove he'd come up with the general look—perhaps particularly the distinctive mask—before Bill. Yet in the same book, he credited Bill with originating Batman's design, bat cowl and all.

★★★

In 1966 Batman became the first costumed hero to get a show on prime-time network TV. (The 1950s series *The Adventures of Superman* had been syndicated, airing at different times on different stations.) Bill co-wrote a two-part *Batman* episode with Charles Sinclair, a longtime friend and writing partner with whom he had collaborated on scripts for radio shows, TV dramas, and B movies. "Bill was the envy of his [comic-book] colleagues when he and I cracked into *Batman* because he was the only guy from that particular circle who made it [to the TV show]," Charles said.

The Batman television show made Bob wealthy. The 1989 Batman movie flashed the credit line "Based on Batman characters created by Bob Kane" to audiences worldwide. Bob died in 1998, twenty-four years after Bill.

Batman is perhaps the most lucrative superhero in history. At most any point, he headlines more monthly comic books than any other DC Comics character. Similarly, more action figures have been made of him than any other DC character—hundreds more than his closest competitor, Superman. He has starred in first-run television animation since 1968 and almost continuously since 1992. The 2008 film *The Dark Knight* broke numerous records, including biggest opening day of all time. (Incidentally, that now-famous "Dark Knight" nickname first appeared in 1940 in *Batman* #1—in a story Bill wrote.)

At present DC cannot legally add Bill's name to the credit line for Batman, but plenty of respected DC employees and associates have said or implied that it should be there. Here are just a few:

- Julius Schwartz, beloved DC editor from 1944 to 1986, called Bill the "best scripter in the business and the true co-creator of Batman."
- Paul Levitz, a DC writer who went on to serve as the president of the company from 2002 to 2009, wrote in *Detective Comics* #500 (1981) that Batman was "the creation of Bob Kane and Bill Finger."
- Carmine Infantino, a pioneering DC artist who became the company's publisher from 1971 to 1976, told me, "You ought to call [your book] *The Father of Batman*. You wouldn't be wrong."

And Jerry Robinson, who began working with Bill and Bob shortly after Batman's debut, said, "[Bill] had more to do with the molding of Batman than Bob. He just did so many things at the beginning, . . . creating almost all the other characters, . . . the whole persona, the whole temper, the . . . origin of Batman." In another interview, he was even more direct: "Bill Finger deserves co-credit for the creation of Batman, simple as that."

Bob's greatest talent may have been the ability to recognize other talent. His greatest flaw may have been the inability to honor that talent.

Bill's greatest flaw may have been the inability to defend his talent. His greatest talent was the ability to forge legends.

Simple as that.

Finding Finger

Bill Finger brought out the detective in Batman, and also in me.

I began researching this book in 2006. My first two goals: find photos and find family. With conviction, insiders in the comics industry told me the following:

1. Only two photos of Bill exist.
2. Even if there were Batman royalties for Bill, he left no heir.

Yet after contacting more than two hundred people nationwide, including comic-book writers and artists, librarians, genealogists, Bronx historians, college professors, former army personnel, funeral-home managers, cemetery administrators, gay and lesbian organization leaders, cooking-magazine editors, television producers, a high-school principal, a clergyman, a diner owner, a hippie musician, and what feels like eighty people over the age of eighty . . .

I found that neither statement is true.

First, five photos of Bill have been published. The first two were printed only once, generations ago; both were grainy. The first ran in 1941, in *Green Lantern* #1—Bill co-created him, too. The second was in a 1965 New York comic convention schedule. Many comics people either don't know about those two or don't count them due to their poor quality. The third and fourth photos show Bill in profile and in shadow, respectively. The fifth picture (a group shot of Bill and other comics luminaries at a dinner circa 1945) surfaced in the 2008 book *The DC Vault*.

But when people told me only two photos of Bill exist, what they really meant was only two were *known* to exist.

From seven sources over nine months, I found eleven more.

The photos span Bill's adult life. All are black and white. They come from an eclectic assortment of people that the comics community didn't know about: Bill's niece on his first wife's side, his first wife's cousin, his *second* wife, his second wife's son, the second wife of Bill's writing partner Charles Sinclair, . . . and Bill's only grandchild. (More on this to come.)

Before finding these people, I started with an obvious source: Bill's (and Bob's) alma mater, DeWitt Clinton High School in the Bronx.

The school put me in touch with Gerard Pelisson, its de facto and supremely knowledgeable historian. Gerard was keen for the quest, though he did warn me he had already looked without luck for record of Bill. In June 2006 we combed through yellowed yearbooks from 1930 through 1934, seeing some Fingers but no Bill Finger.

Around this time I'd learned that Bill and his first wife, Portia, had divorced and that Bill had remarried in the late 1960s. Lyn Simmons, Bill's second wife—vivid well into her eighties and deeply moved that someone was writing about Bill—mentioned something she at first didn't want me to publish but has since given her blessing for. Bill's given name was not William. It was Milton. (He hated it.)

I told Gerard, but as an aside. We continued to correspond about other things. Then six months later, he emailed with the subject line "Not to get your hopes up, but . . ." Attached was a photo from the June 1933 yearbook of a Milton Finger. I don't know if that was a Finger we had passed over, and I really don't know why it hadn't occurred to me to recheck the yearbooks as soon as I learned about *Milton*. But it was indeed him, now the earliest known photo of Bill Finger.

According to Milton Finger's high school yearbook, he was on the Art Squad, was nicknamed "Tink," and was planning to be a doctor. (1933)

"We weren't photo people," Lyn told me. She did have one photo of Bill—in silhouette. However, Steve Simmons, Lyn's son from a previous marriage, also had a photo of Bill— somewhere. Eight months later he found it. It was worth the wait, because it's the clearest shot I've uncovered (and, quirkily, one of three I found in which Bill is shirtless).

In a wild coincidence Steve and I lived in the same town at the time, meaning that for years, an undiscovered photo of Bill Finger was essentially around the corner from me.

After Lyn I felt there was no one else to find whose existence could thrill me as intensely.

I was wrong.

★★★

What I consider the best of the "new" Bill Finger photos is also the most unlikely. He's not only bare-chested, but also doing yard work. In trousers. (approximately early 1960s)

At comic conventions and on message boards, fans regularly speculate about (or lament the lack of) a Finger heir. In the two interviews he gave about his father, Fred Finger revealed little about his own adult life. He died in 1992 at age forty-three. It is no wonder people say with certainty that no one is left to fight for Finger.

The only paperwork in Fred's file at the Brooklyn surrogate's court was a two-page document detailing what to do with Fred's belongings. The only person named there was a Charles Shaheen.

I traced Shaheen to a small town in North Carolina and learned that he'd passed away in 2002. The lone funeral home there wouldn't divulge much, but did tell me where he had worked. One of Shaheen's coworkers told me she had helped clean out Shaheen's place after his death—and found stubs of Batman checks from DC Comics.

Bill had begun to receive modest reprint royalties at the end of his life, but because he had no *official* stake in Batman, I was surprised that royalties were still being paid almost thirty years later. Shaheen's coworker thought the money probably ended with Shaheen, but said there was a guy named Jesse Maloney who used to spend a lot of time with him. Maloney was a drifter. I couldn't find him.

In February 2007, after squinting through hundreds of scanned obituaries in the *New York Times* online, I finally hit another of the names I was looking for: Portia Finger, Bill's first wife and Fred's mother. But the obituary was for Portia's mother. After fruitless months of scouring ancestry sites and requesting birth certificates, I finally learned the names of Portia's (deceased) twin and her two children, Eric and Judy. Their last name was uncommon, so I easily found numbers for both. It was late on the East Coast, where I was, but Eric was out west, so I phoned him right then.

"This guy's asking about Uncle Bill!" he called to his wife. "No one's ever asked about Uncle Bill before." He said his sister had family photos. Then came the biggest blindside of my research.

"Have you talked with Bill's granddaughter?"

Granddaughter?

How could that be?

Fred was an only child and was gay, with no known history of adopting.

The next day, Judy explained. It turned out that Fred had been married to a woman for a short time—and they had a daughter. She was named after the Greek goddess of wisdom and war: Athena.

Bill Finger *did* have a living heir after all.

Neither Eric nor Judy had contact information for Athena, but I tracked her down on MySpace, where her profile indicated that her dog's name was Bruce Wayne.

I emailed her, and that day, she called. She was born two years after Bill died, so she had no firsthand stories of him, but she shared what her father had told her.

It became clear that Fred's final days had been extremely hard on her. On top of the pain of losing her dad, Athena had to accept that the inheritor named in the settlement of Fred's estate had been not her, but rather Charles Shaheen. Fifteen years later she was emotional that the subject had come up again. Overall, however, Athena struck me as grounded, bright, and strongly interested in learning more about her grandfather. She immediately felt like my own family—or rather, I somehow felt like a part of hers.

Bill could drive a plot but not a car—he never even got a driver's license—so either Portia drove them to Cape Cod (shown here) or they took public transportation. (1940s)

I learned that Shaheen had been Fred's partner, whom the family had disapproved of. Athena was shocked that he had been getting royalties—and that he had died. She'd heard from DC after her father passed away, but only once, and she had not received any money. I suggested she contact the company. She hesitated. I nudged. She decided to try it.

A lawyer at DC told Athena that the company had been sending royalties to Jesse Maloney, who had (falsely) claimed to be Fred's brother. The lawyer asked if Athena could prove her relationship to Fred. One submitted birth certificate later, DC rerouted all Bill Finger royalties to his only grandchild.

The money can't approach what Bob Kane's estate has received, but to the working mother of a young son, it was welcome. And it may be as close to a happy ending as Bill Finger will ever get. He just didn't live long enough to experience it.

Notes

Detective Comics #27, which included the first Batman story, was the May 1939 issue. However, comic books (then and now) hit stands in advance of their cover dates. According to house ads in later issues of *Detective,* the title went on sale "about the 5th of every month." Since Bill and Bob created Batman in early 1939, March seems too early for his debut, so I went with April.

All dialogue is excerpted from interviews and other primary sources. Some information comes from my conversations with people who knew Bill personally, including Lyn Simmons, Charles Sinclair, Bonnie Burrell, Judy Flam, Tom Fagan, Jerry Bails, Arnold Drake, Jerry Robinson, Alvin Schwartz, and Carmine Infantino.

The wordplay with *bill, finger,* and *bat* in this book is an homage: Bill was known to use puns in his Batman stories.

Selected Bibliography

Alter Ego, no. 20 (Jan. 2003). Various articles about 1965 New York Comicon.

Amazing World of DC Comics. "In Memoriam: William Finger (1914–1974)." No. 1 (July–Aug. 1974): 28.

Bails, Jerry. "If the Truth Be Known or 'A Finger in Every Plot!'" One-page supplement to *CAPA-alpha,* no. 12 (Sept. 1965).

"ComiCon." Talk of the Town. *New Yorker,* Aug. 21, 1965, 23–24.

Daniels, Les. *Batman: The Complete History.* San Francisco: Chronicle Books, 1999.

David Anthony Kraft's Comics Interview Super Special. "Batman: Real Origins of the Dark Knight." Jan. 1989.

Fagan, Tom. "Bill Finger—Man Behind a Legend." Unpublished article based on an interview with Bill Finger, 1965.

Finger, Bill. "The Case of the Chemical Syndicate." *Detective Comics,* no. 27 (May 1939). Reprinted in *The Batman Chronicles,* vol. 1, 4–9. New York: DC Comics, 2005.

Finger, Bill. Interview by Robert Porfirio. Conducted circa May 1972. Unpublished at the time of writing, but since published in *Creators of the Superheroes,* by Thomas Andrae, 85–89. Neshannock, PA: Hermes Press, 2011.

Finger, Bill. Unpublished letter to Tom Fagan. Oct. 17, 1965.

Finger, Fred. "Fred Finger." Interview by Dwight Jon Zimmerman. *David Anthony Kraft's Comics Interview Super Special,* Jan. 1989. Reprinted in *Alter Ego: The Comic Book Artist Collection,* 140–45. Raleigh, NC: TwoMorrows, 2001.

Green Lantern. "Introducing Bill Finger and Marty Nodell Creators of Green Lantern!" No. 1 (Fall 1941).

Infantino, Carmine. Untitled note. *Famous 1st Edition: Batman No. 1,* vol. 1, no. F-5 (Feb.–Mar. 1975): inside front cover.

Kane, Bob. "An Open Letter to All 'Batmanians' Everywhere." *Batmania Annual* (1967): 25–30.

Kane, Bob. *Batman & Me.* With Tom Andrae. Forestville, CA: Eclipse Books, 1989.

McLauchlin, Jim. "Unmasking Batman." *Wizard,* no. 135 (Dec. 2002): 84–90.

Robinson, Jerry. "Look Out, Batman! It's the Jerry Robinson Interview!" Interview by Gary Groth. *Comics Journal,* no. 271 (Oct. 2005): 72–111.

Schwartz, Alvin. "After the Golden Age." World Famous Comics. www.worldfamouscomics.com/alvin/.

Schwartz, Julius. Batman's Hot-Line. *Detective Comics,* no. 327 (May 1964).

Schwartz, Julius. *Man of Two Worlds: My Life in Science Fiction and Comics.* With Brian M. Thomsen. New York: HarperEntertainment, 2000.

Steranko, James. *The Steranko History of Comics.* Vol. 1. Reading, PA: Supergraphics, 1970.

For a full list of sources, visit **www.charlesbridge.com/BilltheBoyWonder**.

Dear people,

   I come up here as a guest. Is Jerry hospitable? He is not! He goes out of his way to beat me at darts. I go home with a heavy heart.

               Bill Finger

P.S. I just beat him.

P.P.S. Now I'm light again.

This is the only known note in Bill's handwriting. It's from the guest book that Jerry Robinson had in his apartment (circa 1942)

"Bill was the greatest comics writer of his time,
and maybe since."
—Jerry Robinson

"Bill Finger was the genius of comics."